HELP! MOM! THERE ARE LIBERALS UNDER MY BED!

A Small Lesson in Conservatism

By Katharine DeBrecht

Illustrated by Jim Hummel

Published by World Ahead Publishing, Inc., Los Angeles, CA

World Ahead Publishing's books are available at special discounts for bulk purchases. World Ahead Publishing also publishes books in electronic formats. For more information, visit www.worldahead.com.

First Edition

ISBN 0-9767269-0-4
LCCN 2005926354

Printed in China

For J, L & T
My three sweet little inspirations
Keep making me proud

Tommy and Lou were brothers who lived in a small house, on a small street, in a small neighborhood, in a small city, in the great USA.

And, like most good boys, they ate most of their vegetables, did their chores, tried not to fight over their toys, and said their prayers at bedtime — sometimes a little fast if they were extra tired.

But Tommy and Lou had a problem. Each day after building sandcastles in their small sandbox, they would stretch out on a small patch of grass in their backyard and dream of a swing set. And each day they pleaded with their Mom and Dad for a new swing set.

But, Mom and Dad always told the boys that having everything given to them would not make them feel good about themselves, and that earning things on their own would make them feel proud and become better people.

"Oh, how I wish we could have a swing set like some other kids," Lou moaned. Why can't WE get one?"

"Swing sets are an expensive toy," their Mom explained. "Would you love it more if we just gave it to you or if you worked hard for it?"

"Ohh," Lou complained, "What can we do to earn that much money? It just doesn't seem fair..."

But his Mom put her arm around her son and smiled and said "Son, if life gives you lemons, make lemonade."

That gave Tommy an idea.

In the middle of their backyard grew a beautiful lemon tree with hundreds of ripe lemons on each outstretched branch.

"We'll make lemonade and sell it!" Tommy told Lou. "Then we will have enough money to buy our swing set."

The boys were excited, almost too excited to sleep. But they went on to bed, and soon after fell asleep like the good little boys they were.

As they began to dream about their lemonade stand a strange thing happened.

The boys both had the very same, very strange dream about a very strange place called Liberaland.

In their dream, Tommy and Lou worked hard to start their lemonade stand.

They worked hours and hours, day and night, trying to get their recipe just right. Their little hands ached from squeezing lemons and little Lou even got a blister.

But, when they finally got their recipe just right, not too sweet, not too sour, they opened up their stand.

And each day, after school, after homework, after chores, the boys went on squeezing lemons, selling lemonade with smiles and thank-yous, like the good little boys they were.

People LOVED Tommy and Lou's lemonade!

They lined the streets everyday to buy a glass.

"25 cents what a bargain!"

"Not too sweet!"

"Not too sour!"

"The best ever!"

Just like Mom and Dad said, the boys were proud of their hard work, and felt good about taking responsibility to earn the money for their swing set. They were also very happy that their hard work made the stand a success.

"Soon we'll have enough money to buy our swing set!" Lou danced. "I almost feel my feet swinging in the breeze!"

"Wait," Tommy stopped Lou. "Remember Mom and Dad always tell us to help others? We should save some money for less fortunate kids."

"Like kids with no shoes," Lou cheered. "Yes!"

So each day, after school, after homework, after chores, the boys went on squeezing lemons, selling lemonade with smiles and thank-yous, and saving a little extra money for the children with no shoes, like the good little boys they were.

Until one day, a liberal appeared from behind their lemon tree.

"Helllloo," the liberal's eyes grew wide as he gazed at the boys' money. "My, my, boys, you sure have sold a lot of lemonade."

"Oh, yes!" beamed Lou. "And we still have enough..."

"Yes, well," the liberal drummed his fingers on his belly. "I am Mayor Leach of Liberaland," he held out his meaty hand, "Have you paid your tax?"

"Tax?" Tommy asked. "What is that?"

"Well," the liberal's red cheeks smiled, "That is where you give the government half of your money so we can spend it better."

"But we give our extra money for the children with no shoes and we worked so hard," Lou cried. "Look at my blister!"

"Ahh, silly lad," Mayor Leach patted the small boy's head. "How sweet, but you know, we liberals know what is best for our shoeless children."

"Besides," the liberal winked, "why work hard when you can have the government provide for you?"

"Boo-yah!" Mayor Leach grabbed the bag of cash with half of the boy's money.

"Now," he wiped his sweaty brow, "I am late for a press conference," and he disappeared behind the tree.

So each day, after school, after homework, after chores, Tomy and Lou went on squeezing lemons, selling lemonade with smiles and thank-yous, and saved a little extra money for the children with no shoes, and paid half of their money for the tax, like the good little boys they were.

Later that night, while the boys were squeezing lemons, they heard a familiar voice on TV.

"Yes, you see," Mayor Leach stood up big and tall in front of the camera. "We liberals know how to take care of our children with no shoes," his red cheeks glowing on the screen. "That is why I want to announce today that I have purchased three million, yes, THREE MILLION dustpans for our shoeless children."

"Dustpans?" Lou shook his head.

Tommy and Lou felt bad that the shoeless kids would have dustpans, not shoes, and hoped their little extra money would help them buy shoes.

But Tommy and Lou were thankful for the success of their stand; that the rainy days didn't keep customers away; and that Mom and Dad let them stay up one hour later to squeeze lemons. But they were most thankful for the beautiful lemon tree that God had provided them. So atop their stand, they hung a picture of Jesus.

Until one day another liberal appeared from behind their lemon tree.

"Boys, that picture mussst come down!" the liberal hissed as he slid up to the stand.

"But we are thankful..." Lou trailed off.

"No butssssss, little man," the lanky liberal wagged his finger at the two. "You see, I am Mr. Fussman of the LCLU," he leaned forward on the stand, "and my friend, Mr. Afflue, who lives across town happens to see this picture while riding in his limousine on his way home from work, and quite frankly, young man, it offends him!"

"But it is my picture of Jesus on our stand," Tommy began to cry.

"Ah, well, uh, I do have something else you could hang up," the liberal reached into a large bag, "because we liberals are NOT against free speech."

And with that, he hung a picture of a big toe atop their stand. "Hooh-hah" Mr. Fussman whistled, wearing a big smile.

"A big toe?" Lou winced.

"Well, uh, yes, you see," the liberal twitched his mustache. "According to our research, a big toe is one of only two things that do not offend anyone."

"Now," Mr. Fussman tipped his hat, "I must be going. You see, important people, like me, have important things to do, like being on TV."

"No praying here either, boys!" he called over his shoulder as he disappeared behind the tree.

So each day, after school, after homework, after chores, the boys went on squeezing lemons, selling lemonade with smiles and thank-yous, and saved a little extra money for the children with no shoes, and paid half of their money for the tax, and prayed quietly with a big toe atop their stand, like the good little boys they were.

Until one day in their strange dream, another liberal appeared from behind their lemon tree.

"Now you listen here! I am Congresswoman Clunkton," the liberal huffed "and as I was peeking in the Johnsons' window the other night, I saw Mrs. Johnson excuse her son, George, from the table before eating his vegetables!" The liberal sighed and rolled her eyes. "Tsk, tsk, parents."

"But I thought George had the flu and his Mom was making him some soup," Lou whispered to Tommy.

"Now we have just passed a law about this," Ms. Clunkton beamed. "You see, parents just don't know how to make sure their children eat their vegetables!" She threw her hands on her hips and rolled her eyes. "It takes a village to get kids to eat their vegetables!"

"Sooo," Ms. Clunkton pounded her fist on the stand, "for every glass of lemonade you sell, you must, I say, you MUST give two pieces of broccoli with it."

"Broccoli, yuck!" cried Tommy. "Why would people want broccoli with their lemonade?"

"Be glad it's not lima beans, son," the liberal glared at Tommy. "Now, I have a fundraising event in a few minutes," she announced, fluffing her hair in a glass.

"By the way," Ms. Clunkton turned back towards the boys, "as of Monday, Senator Kruckle from Taxachussetts is sponsoring a sugar law — rots kids' teeth, you know, so only one teaspoon of sugar allowed."

Tommy and Lou tried their best to smile at the bossy liberal as she ducked back behind the tree, and called out to the boys, "May make the lemonade sour, but we know what is best!" But as soon as she disappeared behind the tree, the boys quietly, and somewhat disappointedly, got back to selling lemonade.

So each day, after school, after homework, after chores, the boys went on squeezing lemons, selling lemonade with smiles and thank-yous, and saved a little extra money for the children with no shoes, and paid half of their money for the tax, and prayed quietly with a big toe atop their stand, and gave out two pieces of broccoli with each glass with only one teaspoon of sugar, like the good little boys they were.

Tommy and Lou noticed that there were fewer customers at their lemonade stand. The lemonade had become sour from the sugar laws, piles of uneaten broccoli were left in the trash and some kids hid behind their parents when they saw the big toe atop the boys' stand.

Nonetheless, Tommy and Lou worked twice as hard with bigger smiles and extra thank yous to save their stand.

Until one day, all the liberals started streaming out from behind the lemon tree with cameras flashing and microphones whirling, shouting:

"More taxes! More dustpans!"

"No one is eating their vegetables!"

"I heard praying!"

"You do not know how to run this stand, we can do it better!"

Just then a tall liberal pushed his way in front of the microphones.

"Twenty-five cents a glass is an outrage!" Senator Kruckle shook his fist at the cameras. "Two million people each day go without lemonade and half of our children are not eating their vegetables! AND we have a rotting teeth epidemic!" The liberal glared into the cameras, "It is greed, pure greed."

"But we worked hard for this stand," Tommy cried, "and people used to like our lemonade before all your silly rules."

"This is mean-spiritedness," Senator Kruckle shook his head and waved his hands over the boys. "Today, my proud liberals, we have passed a new law," his eyes sparkled in the flashing cameras. "According to the new Boxster-Teddy-Algore-Juffords-Paloosi-Byrdie-Waxball-Deanie-Schooner Law, all lemonade stands are now property of liberals."

And with that, the liberals took over Tommy and Lou's stand.

And each day, after press conferences, after TV bookings and after limousine rides, the liberals sold sour lemonade for $5.00 a glass, with you-betters and you-don'ts, and each day bought more dustpans for the shoeless children, and lectured loudly with a big toe atop their stand, and gave out more broccoli than anyone would eat, like the liberals that they were.

Tommy and Lou finally awoke from their long and strange dream.

"Why, Tommy?" Lou rubbed his eyes and yawned. "Why should we work so hard when liberals might tell us what to do and take everything away?"

"Dad always says to work hard and do our best." Tommy shrugged.

"What if all those liberals try to stop us again?" Lou looked worried.

"Just be glad we're not in Liberaland anymore," Tommy smiled at Lou. "We still can earn the money for our swing set if we work hard."

"Come on," Tommy pulled his brother out of bed. "I bet we get that swing set by the end of summer."

And off they went to start squeezing lemons,
like the good little conservatives they were.

Cast of Characters

The cranky Liberals are gone for now, but they'll soon be back with more taxes, more big toes, and even more dustbins!

Be on the lookout for future *Help! Mom!* adventures in stores soon, and visit our Web site at www.helpmombooks.com for special bonus material.

In the meantime, enjoy the following profiles of the dastardly Liberals...

TAX LIBERAL

Mayor Leach has served as Mayor of Liberaland for 20 years. A multimillionaire, he earned his money the old-fashioned liberal way—he married into it. His wife, Allmine, is heiress to the great Dustpans, Inc. fortune. His three children, following in the footsteps of their parents, attend the prestigious Liberaland Elite Academy for Special People. Mayor Leach's accomplishments include passing a 50% tax rate on the "rich" (anyone who earns enough to buy more than three glasses of lemonade every year, except wage earners in a specified cleaning field) and using taxpayers' money to build 163 roads and 82 bridges that are named after him.

BIG TOE LIBERAL

Mr. Fussman is the founder of the LCLU (Liberaland Civil Liberties Union), a group that used the courts to sue Christians to get all crosses removed from sight and replaced with Big Toes, which, according to polls, do not offend anyone. Churches are now required to resemble strip malls. The LCLU was also able to have a Liberaland judge order that the pledge of allegiance be changed to the words from "Itsy, Bitsy Spider." Mr. Fussman is known to be fond of saying, "We don't need laws, just judges." In an upcoming edition of the Help! Mom! series, he will reveal what the "other thing" that offends no one is.

BROCCOLI LIBERAL

Congresswoman Clunkton is a star in the Liberaland Socialist Party (LSP) and a multimillionaire from class action lawsuits. She once sued the hamburger chain MacBurgers, Inc. for $50 gazillion, claiming that the citizens of Liberaland were not told that eating 200 cheeseburgers per day could make them fat. Now that she is in the Liberaland Congress, Rep. Clunkton has written a law to require all pencil manufacturers to spend billions of dollars to attach a tag to pencils with the warning "Warning! Don't Poke in Your Eye." She also intends to write laws making it illegal to eat peanut butter and jelly sandwiches, watch cartoons, or stay up after 7:30 pm.

TALL LIBERAL

Senator Kruckle from Taxachussetts is a former Presidential candidate and comes from a long line of Kruckles in politics. Because of his family name, he has earned millions from fundraising and speaking engagements and has never had to work at a real job. He is the author of the Greedy Business Law, which requires all Liberaland companies to give their employees eleven months of vacation time every year. Senator Kruckle is well known for demanding that the Girl Scouts only sell cookies made from spinach and onions. He is famous for saying, "Ask not what I can do for you, ask what the government can do for me."

SPECIAL THANKS to my illustrator, Jim, for doing a great job, to Greg Allen for being a wonderful mentor, to Eric and Norman at World Ahead for making this experience way too much fun, to my family and friends who cheered me on. Very special thanks to my husband for his continued and amazing support.

THANKS also to all those silly liberals who helped me become more conservative and made writing this book so much fun. I am sure they'll be pleased that around fifty percent of the proceeds of this book will go to taxes.

About the Author: Katharine DeBrecht is the pen name for a mother of three. A freelance newspaper reporter who graduated cum laude from Saint Mary's College in Notre Dame, she served as South Carolina's co-captain of "Security Moms for Bush."

About the Illustrator: Jim Hummel is a professional illustrator and instructor at San Jose State University. A military veteran and former art director for the Associated Press, he is a past winner of the prestigious Reuben Award from the National Cartoonists Society.